# Mary, Juma and Simba the dog

**Helen Day and Chitra Parvathy Merchant**

This book was co-funded by

DFID Department for International Development

A1095273

act:onaid

Mary and Juma loved
their puppy Simba,
but he was always in trouble.

Early on Saturday morning he stuck his nose in a pot of *ugali*.

"I'll paddle your backside when I catch you," cried their mother.

Then he ate a plastic sandal.
"He deserves to be sick,"
said Jeffrey, their older brother.

After breakfast he chewed Mary's chalk board. "Oh Simba, what will I write my sums on now?" she sighed.

At lunchtime their
mother's bead necklace
disappeared.

"That puppy is to
blame for sure,"
she stormed.

"He will have to go

8

"Hubble, bubble, the dog's in trouble,"

sang the *ekegonkoru* bird in its croaky voice.

Simba gazed at Mary with his maize-yellow eyes. "Where have you put it, you silly dog?" she asked.

"Let's follow him," said Juma. "Perhaps we'll find out."

Outside, Simba jumped up
at Auntie Rita and tore her new *kanga*.

"That dog should
mind his manners"
she yelled crossly.

The children followed Simba through the dusty streets of Ziwa La Ng'ombe. Soon they came to the Mombasa road.

A matatu hooted loudly

ust missed the careless puppy.

houted,

"here, Simba,"

but he was off again, tail flying like a kite.

When they passed Mr Amokoya's café,
Simba spotted a cat and dashed inside.

"Just when Mathare United were about
to score!" complained the customers.

school

Sim

Outside their school
some friends
were playing
football.

"No you don'
said Juma.

ed the ball.

WEAVER BIRD

NeST

HOrn BILL NeST

At midday, Simba and the children rested under the big, old baobab tree. The sun shone through the leaves making pretty shapes on their legs.

"It's hopeless," said Juma.

"We'll never find the necklace."

His sister closed her
eyes and then snapped
them open again.

"What's that?"
she cried.

High up in the
baobab tree she
spied a glint of red
and green glass.

"Quick, Juma,"
she said,
"give me a leg-up."

It was hard to climb the tree, but Mary clung on until she reach

...hole hidden by twigs and leaves.

"Come up, brother," she gasped.

23

The stolen
necklace
sparkled
in the hole!

Next to it lay a metal comb,
two bangles, some keys and
a small oil lamp.

" think I know who put these here,"
said Juma.

When they got home, their mother was buying water from Silvano.

"We've found your necklace!" said Mary happily.

"And there's the thief!" added Juma, pointing to the ekegonkoru bird.

Their mother agreed that Simba could stay. Simba wagged his tail in reply.

"As for that bird," she laughed, "he'll have to go."

"Kai, kaaaai," croaked the bird.

"If you can catch me!"

# Animals

**Chameleon** The chameleon tries to hide by changing colour to match its background.

**Ekegonkoru bird** Ekegonkoru birds are always on the look-out for shiny objects to steal, just like magpies. Ekegonkoru is the Kisii name for the bird. Some of the people in Ziwa are from the Kisii tribe.

**Giraffe** Giraffes live on the plains of Kenya.

**Hornbill** Hornbills nest in a hole in a baobab tree. The female then gets inside and closes the hole with mud. She leaves a small opening for her beak so she can take food from the male.

**Mouse** Mice live in towns and are always on the look-out for food.

**Snake** The boomslang snake makes its home in the baobab tree. Its bite is poisonous.

**Weaver bird** The busy weaver bird works hard to make a hanging nest.

As well as Simba the dog, you will find a cow, a goat, a cat and some chickens in the book!

# Glossary

**Baobab** Baobab trees can grow very big and live a long time. They are hollow in the middle. The baobab tree in Ziwa is 200 years old. Once men came to the tree to pray for strength and to leave gifts in its hollows. Now meetings are held under the tree.

**Handcart** Water sellers like Silvano in the story, use hand-carts to take big cans full of water to their customers. Handcarts are also used to carry goods.

**Kanga** The skirt worn by Auntie Rita is popular with many women in Kenya. Kangas are very colourful and may be printed with a proverb, or saying, in Swahili.

**Mango** There are mango trees all over Mombasa. Children love to eat the sweet, juicy fruit. The mango trees outside the school in Ziwa are a popular place for playing games.

**Matatu** A matatu is a minibus that takes people around the city. Matatus drive fast and fit in as many passengers as possible. They play loud music as they go.

**Ugali** Ugali is maize flour and water mashed together. It is cooked outside over a wood fire. Juma and Mary eat ugali every day with meat, fish or vegetables.

The menu at Mr Amokoya's video café

| | Kenyan Shillings |
|---|---|
| Maziwa (milk) | 15 |
| Chai special (spicy tea) | 15 |
| Rangi (black tea) | 7 |
| Soda ndogo (fizzy drink) | 16 |
| Chapati | 10 |
| Githeri (maize and beans) | 25 |
| Sukuma (kale) | 15 |
| Cabbage | 15 |
| Eggs-fry | 25 |
| Ugali | 15 |

£1 = 114 Kenyan shillings (May 2002).

**Numbers**

| 1 | moja |
|---|---|
| 2 | mbili |
| 3 | tatu |
| 4 | nne |
| 5 | tano |

## Swahili

Jambo - Hello

Kwaheri - Goodbye

Tafadhali - Please

Hapana - No

Ndiyo - Yes

Sawa sawa - OK

Ahsante (sana) - Thank you (very much)

# More information

**The story** Mary, Juma and Simba the dog is set in Ziwa La Ng'ombe (Ziwa), near Mombasa, a city on the coast of Kenya. It means 'Lake of Cattle' in Swahili. Swahili is the main language of Kenya.

Some children who live here do not go to school. This is because their parents cannot pay the school fees. Or children may need to work to help buy food for their families. At school, children use chalk boards instead of paper and pens, which cost too much money. ActionAid is working with the community of Ziwa.